TogetherVerse

written and illustrated by
Esther Samuels-Davis

At the picnic there was a big splat.

"What is that?" asked Isabel.

A whole bowl of the night sky had splashed right onto Isabel's shirt.

"Ooo," cooed the Jasmine flowers. "Look at all the sparkling stars in there."

"The night sky is such a marvelous part of our world," said the lizard.

Isabel was curious. "What does it mean to be part of our world?" she asked.

A bird flying high above heard Isabel's question.

"The world is made of many parts," said the bird. "Up here in the clouds I can see lots of big things below."

"What do you see?" Isabel called to the bird.

"I can see creatures in the ocean and houses on the hilltops. There are forests and mountains and sandy shores far away."

"But those things are much bigger than me," Isabel said. "Can I be a part of the world even though I am so small?"

8

Isabel felt a tap on her fingertip.

"I am a part of the world," peeped the little red bug. "And I am much smaller than you. Down here blades of grass are as tall as trees! I see pebbles like boulders and flowers that tower high above my head. We are all a part of the world, no matter how small or big we are."

"Don't you feel lonely being so small?" Isabel asked.

"Nobody is ever all alone," bubbled the water.

"I am not lonely." The fish waved its tail back and forth. "You, water, are always around me! You lift me up and help me swim fast."

"And thanks to all these tall plants I can build my web to catch my lunch," grinned the spider hungrily. "If we were not here together, my belly would be grumbling."

"My toes together help me stand tall and climb high!" said the red bug.

"You mean the ten little friends on the bottom of my feet?" exclaimed Isabel.

"Look at all these threads in your sweater sleeves," said the spider. "One thread alone would not do much, but woven together they keep you warm."

"*Very* warm indeed," murmured the leaf.

17

"We flowers have oodles of seeds," said the
big yellow dandelion. "Together we cover
whole fields with new blossoms for the bees."

"Wow," smiled Isabel. "You are like one big
colorful neighborhood."

"Up here in the sky we are colorful too," the fluffy rainclouds boomed. "We are not just grey, clouds are made from all the colors of the rainbow."

"Together they brighten up any stormy day," said Isabel, swirling her paintbrush.

21

Isabel closed her eyes.

Then, with a voice like a galaxy of clinking crystals, the splat of the night sky spoke up. "To be part of the world is to feel how powerful we are when we join together."

Isabel felt the warm threads on her arms and the soft grass tickling her toes. She felt the wind carrying seeds to grassy fields and the rumble of faraway clouds giving colors to rainy afternoons.

Isabel felt the world and how it all fits together.

"Here's to the seas, to the mountains and trees!" she cheered. "To the bugs and the flowers, to the toes on our feet. Here's to you. Here's to me. Here's to being a part of this marvelous togetherverse."

"Ooo," cooed the Jasmine flowers. "Look at all of us sparkling stars."

The night sky twinkled up above and the big splat on Isabel's shirt twinkled back.

Together Verse
Written and illustrated by Esther Samuels-Davis
© 2019 taotime verlag

taotime.ch
Kappelen 1
CH-5706 Boniswil
Switzerland

Second Edition
ISBN 978-3-906945-20-0
Book design: Esther Samuels-Davis
Printed in China by Arton Art Printing (HK) Limited

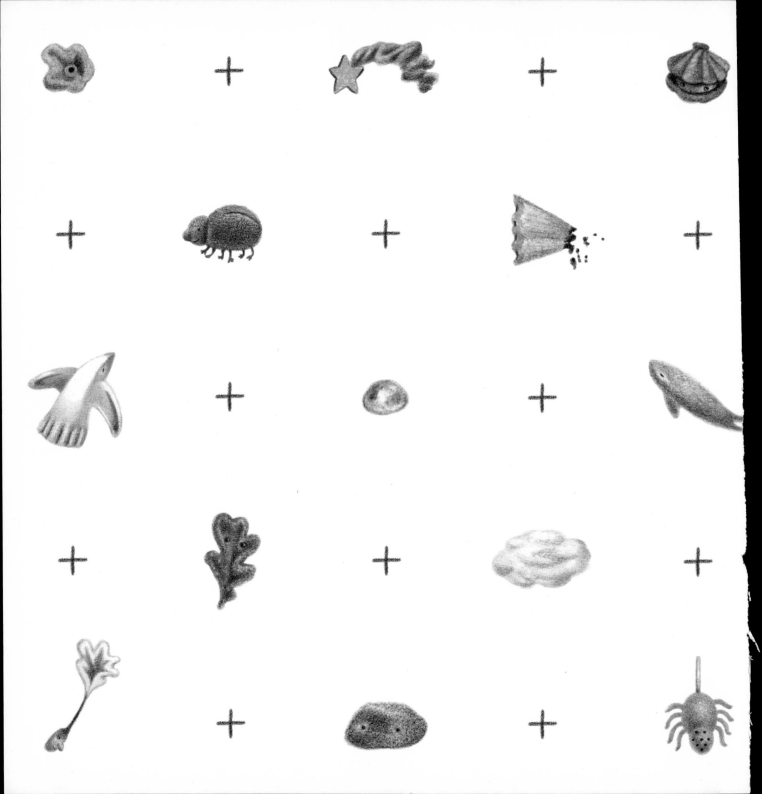